MARRYING THE POSSESSIVE NEIGHBOR

IRIS WEST

To you, my reader. I hope you love Blossom Ford, and the sexy men, curvy women and kind but extremely interfering folk that live there, as much as I do.

CHAPTER ONE

Jasmine

HOW THE HECK am I supposed to choose between pistachio and strawberry ice-cream? I can't. So, I'm having both. Not at the same time; I hate that. With pistachio ice-cream, I stroll to my cozy sitting room.

This is the life I wanted for myself after finishing my nursing degree; helping children get better at work then having lazy downtime watching movies or visiting my favorite places. Mom and Dad are away on a cruise, so I only need to do the bare minimum where housework is concerned.

The only thing missing is a chef to cook delicious meals. Some days, when I've had a hard time at the hospital, it's tiring to cook. Still, there are instant noodles and it's way better than being married fresh out of college like my best friend Nia. A shiver runs through me at the thought of having to give up my freedom as I plonk myself on the plushy, leather sofa.

I hated watching my parents work so hard to take care of me and my sister. They married straight out of high school after finding out Mom was pregnant with my sister. They didn't experience adulthood without the responsibilities marriage and children bring. I promised myself I would travel the world and have fun before I had so many responsibilities.

Qualifying as a registered nurse was the first step toward my goal. In a couple of years, when I've gained enough experience, I can work all over the world and visit the places I've dreamed about.

The sound of a powerful motorcycle makes me pause, the spoonful of ice-cream heading to my mouth. That's something else I'd like to do. Ride a bike. It's a shame the bikers that came to town last year seem a little too scary for me to contemplate befriending them.

I place the ice-cream in my mouth and close my eyes, savoring the ice-cold deliciousness. I reach for the remote control, but before I turn the TV on, I hear what I think is the sound of a motorcycle shutting down. From next door.

I frown. It's Tuesday, the new owner is not moving in till Thursday. Besides, Mrs. Thatcher–the previous owner of the house and my neighbor of twenty-two years, said the new owner is a middle-aged writer. I jump off the couch and pull the curtain open a little.

My heart beats a little faster when I spot a large

motorcycle parked on the front lawn of the neighboring house. I'm five feet ten, so I'm used to tall people, however the man stalking toward the front door is large even to me. He's dressed all in black.

My heart sinks as he bends and does something to the door, his large back blocking my view of the keyhole.

I dial Mrs. Thatcher's number. After the fifth ring, I give up. Somehow, he opened the door. I run to the kitchen, look around for something, anything I can fend off the man if he becomes aggressive. I can't think of anything. The frying pan I used in the morning catches my attention. I grab it and my keys and head next door.

I try to quiet my pounding heart. It's hard to know if my footsteps are silent. Before I open the gate to the house, I dial 911.

"He's lurking around in the darkness. He would have switched on the lights if he were here legitimately," I whisper into my phone when Cal, the young police officer I went to school with, asks if I'm sure it's an intruder.

"For heaven's sake, Jasmine, just go back home and wait. I'll be there soon."

A noise sounds from the inside, like a vase falling and smashing into smithereens. I can't stand out here any longer.

In the yard, I lean down and take a close picture of the bike's plate. Then I creep towards the door, the frying pan held high. I slip past the open door and meet darkness. No wonder the intruder is breaking things.

I debate whether to switch the light on my phone but decide against it. That might alert the thief. Because only one would skulk in the darkness like this. I know the layout of the house very well; it's the same as mine. Swearing noises come from the kitchen, so I head there.

I can just make out his back when I enter the room. He's pointing his phone torch into a cupboard. I move away from the kitchen door, leaving plenty of room for him to run away. Although I'd love to catch him, my safety is more important. I just want to make sure he steals nothing.

I switch on my phone torch and aim it at him with my left hand. With my right, I lift the frying pan and wave it threateningly.

"I called the police. You better leave." I tried strengthening my voice, yet even I can tell it's trembling.

Instead of running, he points his phone towards me. Moves it up and down the length of my body.

"They'll be here any minute now. The police," I say, tensing up, fear a bitter taste in my mouth that only sours when he moves toward me.

"Don't come any closer." I take a step back. And another, mirroring his movement.

He stops. He's even taller than I thought he was. There's an air of strength and agility in the way he moves. The room feels smaller. Is that a smile on his face?

"A Goddess just walked into my house. How am I supposed to keep still?"

I blink. Have I stumbled into a madman? How can he try to flirt with me in such a situation? Does he think I'll fall for this type of sweet talk? Or that I'm bluffing about the police?

"If you don't stop, I'll hit you," I say, brandishing the pan.

"Stay still and put the pan down. Let's talk. The floor has a few shards of glass."

As if I'm going to listen to him. I take another step back. He moves forward. I swing the pan with all my might. Instead of the satisfying thud and yelp I expect to hear, I spin until a powerful arm presses my front flush against the intruder's solid chest and my twists my arm by the side of my body.

My breath whooshes out and I sense the frying pan fall from my nerveless fingers. I try to move away, but nothing happens.

"I'm going to marry you. I will not hurt any bit of these beautiful curves," his voice is a seductive whisper against my neck.

I shiver, unsure if it's from fear alone. Appalled, I try to move out of his arms again.

"I'll let go. I'm not a thief. This is my house."

"Then let me go."

He releases me. I rush away from him and trip over something. My leg gives way. I fall, hard. I hear a

shocked expletive before pain jars my body and I see
stars dance.

CHAPTER TWO

Hunter

THE MOMENT I saw Jasmine, I knew I found the woman I'd been searching for all my adult life, since the moment I decided I would not live alone like Mom. Her beautiful curves, full lips and shinning locs drew my eyes, but I knew for sure when I saw the determined look on her face as she faced me. She was smaller than me, didn't know what I might do to her, however she was willing to protect a neighbor's house from someone she thought was a thief.

That's when I fell for her and knew she was supposed to be mine. I never expected to find the woman of my dreams brandishing what she thought was a weapon against me in a darkened kitchen. Or for her to be so young. She's seventeen years younger than me.

"Mr. Wilson?"

I glance at the young police officer. "Everything checks out, so you're free to go. I'm sorry for the misunderstanding."

I nod at Jasmine. "It's my fault she hurt herself. I'll stay until a family member comes."

"The thing is her parents are away at the moment. I could call her friend or sister, but I don't think she'd want that, not when they live out of town, and it looks like it's nothing too serious. I'll call or pop in when I can to see how she's getting on."

There's more than a concerned cop to citizen relationship between Officer Thomas and Jasmine. There's something in the way he says her name that rings alarm bells inside of me.

"Do you know her well?" I ask.

His eyes drift to the bed where Jasmine is sleeping after he stares at me for a while. He's a few inches shorter than me, but he's bulkier, with a bodybuilder's physique. He looks about twenty-four. "We went to school together. I know her family well, too."

I like the younger man's steady gaze, however; I hope I'm wrong about my suspicions regarding the way he feels about Jasmine.

"I insist on staying."

"She might be a little shocked if she opens her eyes and sees you sitting there. She doesn't yet know you're not a thief."

"I'll get a nurse or doctor straight away."

Officer Thomas gives me another assessing glance, but when his radio beeps, he eventually nods, speaks briefly to a couple of nurses at the nursing station, and leaves the Emergency Room.

I sit back in the chair facing the bed, savor the sound of her name, let my eyes rove over her oval-shaped face, pert nose and beautiful dark brown skin. Her locs are black close to her head, then golden brown at the tips.

Her eyes open. She blinks at the ceiling twice before she looks around the room and her gaze lands on me. Recognition returns. She tries to sit up, winces and lies back. I get Martha, the nurse who'd asked for my autograph earlier.

"Hi sweetheart. Officer Thomas brought you in. You fell? You have a few bruises on your arms and face and your body might be a little sore, but you have broken nothing. We're just waiting on a few results and if everything is fine, you can go home."

Jasmine picks up the remote control beside her and elevates the bed until she's in a sitting position.

"Do you remember what happened?" She looks at me, then back at Jasmine, who nods. "Officer Thomas said to mention he's confirmed Mr. Wilson here is the owner of the house next door." Her lips tug up. "You're so lucky to be living next door to such a famous writer. I'm jealous, to be honest."

Jasmine looks at me. "Writer?"

"Oh my gosh. You must not like thrillers. Mr. Wilson is one of the best phycological thriller authors in the world. And he's one of our own." She pushes her white hair behind her ear and looks at me.

"Thank you nurse Martha. I'd really appreciate if you kept the knowledge that I'm in Blossom Ford a secret for now."

"My mouth is a tomb," she says a line from one of my books.

I'm still humbled by how many people read my books. I started getting used to large book signings in New York, but when people began recognizing me on the streets, I knew it was time to leave and find a quieter place. Of all the places I've been to, none in the US are quieter than Blossom Ford. So, I returned home.

Martha looks at Jasmine. "Let me know if you have questions. Also, if you'd like us to call anyone for you." She checks the observations machine beside the bed, writes something down on the patient notes and moves to the next bed.

"I'm sorry. The new owner is not supposed to move in for a couple of days, so I thought you were a thief. You must have been shocked," Jasmine says.

Her eyes are nearly black. They are huge and dominate her entire face. "I freed up my schedule so came early."

"Why were you moving around in the dark?"

My face heats. I shrug. "I couldn't remember where the electric board was. But it looks like the electricity is turned off, anyway."

The doctor that examined her earlier approaches the bed. "Jasmine. Glad you're awake. You have a mild concussion and some bruises. If you have someone to keep an eye on you for the next twenty-four hours, you can go home tonight."

He looks up from his notes.

"I do," Jasmine says.

My eyebrows shoot up.

"Good. Regarding the soreness in your body, just rest for a couple of days, take some painkillers if you're in any pain. It should sort itself out. Same thing with your sprained ankle. Just rest it." He smiles. "I heard you work in pediatrics, so you know the score."

"Thank you, doctor," Jasmine says and watches him leave before she turns to me.

"Once again, I'm sorry for the trouble I caused. Thank you for coming to the hospital. I guess I'll see you around, since we're neighbors."

"I'll take you home."

Jasmine's smile doesn't reach her eyes. "I'll call my parents. They'll pick me up."

I sit back in the chair. "Aren't they away at the moment?"

Her eyes narrow. She crosses her arms. "Right, I forgot. It must be the fall. My sister will come. I don't want to trouble you any further."

I sit back up. "Jasmine. I don't think your sister is in Blossom Ford either. Or any of your close friends. I'm sure there are people you can call. Blossom Ford is a small town and a few people in the hospital seem to know you, but I don't think you'd want to bother them. Your cop friend said he'll check on you, however I'm guessing he's busy at work and can't stay with you, otherwise he'd be here."

Her arms tighten even more.

"You can't be on your own for a day and I work from home. I feel bad you got hurt. The house owner said she'd tell the neighbors about me, so I think you know a little about me. She definitely told me about the nice family that lives in the adjacent house. She used to take you to kindergarten?"

"Why would Mrs. Thatcher tell you about that?" She ducks her head and reaches for the glass of water on the table beside the bed.

All I'd been interested in was the fact there were no young children in the neighboring house, but now I'm glad part of me was listening to Mrs. Thatcher's gossip.

"I also need a place to stay. In the morning, I can get the electricity switched back on or buy candles. I'll be working the whole night, so I just need to use a kitchen. We don't need to see each other if you'd prefer it that way. Just tell me you're okay now and then. You can also tell your cop friend what's happening."

Jasmine stares at me. Then she nods.

CHAPTER THREE

Jasmine

BRIGHT LIGHT HITS my windows. I know it must be around nine, but I don't want to open my eyes. The smell of coffee causes my nose to twitch.

I bolt upright. Pain lances through my ankle and I remember my humiliating fall. Even more humiliating apology to Hunter Wilson. Seriously, how was I to know he'd pushed forward his move? Moving around in the darkness was also suspicious. At that time of the night, how could I think about something like the electricity being off? Honestly, Mrs. Thatcher could be a miser sometimes.

He must be making coffee. And something else. My nose twitches again. Bacon, eggs, and sausages. Honestly, if I were as good at cooking as I was at smelling food, I'd have gourmet meals every day.

I locate the crutch the hospital gave me and gently get out of bed and head to the bathroom. I take care of business and wash up. When I hobble out, Hunter is waiting for me.

I'm grateful I'm leaning on a crutch. It's the first time I'm seeing in good lighting. His widow's peak, hawked nose and sharp features make him attractive; I can't help staring. Until I realize he's checking out my whole body.

I stand with my legs apart, place the crutch in front of me, and fold my arms. "Stop looking at my body." Last night, in hospital, I was dazed by the fall but now I remember him flirting.

"I'm a first aider. I'm making sure, as far as I can, that you're okay."

"You are? A first aider, I mean?" Jeez, I can't even talk properly. What am I, a high school junior having her first crush? Only I don't remember being this embarrassed when I crushed on Cal.

"Yes. I worked as a lifeguard for a while. I haven't updated the certification in the last few years, still I keep up on it as research for my writing."

He stretches his hand. I gaze uncomprehendingly at him.

"Crutch."

"I need it."

"Your ankle will heal faster if you don't put any pressure on it."

Then I remember. Him carrying me upstairs last

night and asking if there was anything I needed. When I shook my head, he'd asked where my pajamas were and didn't leave until I told him and he'd placed a pair on the bed beside me. All in the name of not straining my ankle.

"I'm better this morning. If I'm careful, I should be okay."

Hunter looks at my swollen foot. Then he takes out the crutches from my fingers and places it against the wall. As if I weigh nothing, he picks me up.

"Get the crutch."

"I could have walked." I mumble, but he doesn't seem interested in what I'm saying. He marches downstairs and deposits me in a chair at the kitchen table.

"Coffee? Or would you like something else?"

I want to refuse yet it smells so good, I nod. I'm starving as well. So, when Hunter places a full breakfast and a steaming mug of wonderful smelling black liquid in front of me, all I can do is thank him.

I watch in silence as he serves his own food, tops up a mug he seems to have been using, and sits across from me.

He's still dressed in black, a long-sleeved t-shirt and jeans that fit his body like a glove.

I'm struggling over the fact that he's a writer. How can someone who sits down for a job have such an athletic body? His rugged good looks, longish hair and the way he walks make him look more like a member of a motorcycle club.

I stop myself from moaning at the flavor of the eggs. They are good enough to rival even Mom's. The bacon and sausages are cooked just the way I like them too, well-done but not burned.

"What are you thinking?" He asks.

"Are you a member of the biker club that turned up in town a while ago?"

"No. There are a couple of clubs I'm friends with. Sometimes I ride with them. I heard there's one in town."

"You've never wanted to join?"

Hunter pauses, like it's a question he wants to consider thoroughly. "I've been tempted, but I guess I'm too much of a loner."

I remember what I heard about his family. "I heard you mom still lives here, and you bought the Irwin place for her."

"I guess you know a lot about me, enough that I can start courting you properly."

Coffee goes down the wrong pipe. I cover my mouth as a coughing fit makes my eyes water. Hunter passes me tissues.

"Are you okay?"

"I will be if you stop saying things like that."

Hunter pours me more coffee.

"You're a beautiful woman. I'm just letting you know I like you and wanna to marry you."

I go hot all over. Put my cup down. "We've only just

met!"

One side of his mouth tugs up. "You have heard of love at first sight, right?"

Why does that half-smile make him seem cute and playful? I shake my head and tell myself to concentrate. Hunter Wilson it too good looking for his own sake.

"I'll admit you're handsome in a rough way, but even if I wanted to date seriously, there's no way I'd get married now. I'm only twenty-two, for heaven's sake! And you can't blurt things like that. You keep it to yourself until you know what the other person is thinking."

Hunter pushes away his empty plate and stares at me with steepled fingers. As if he's trying to figure me out.

"What do you want to do before you get married?"

There's such an earnest look about him, like he really cares. "I want to travel the world. I've only just qualified and started working as a nurse. Once I've gained enough experience, in maybe a year or two, I plan to work in other countries and get to know the world that way. It won't cost too much then."

"How would marrying me stop you from doing that?"

"Seriously? How can I traipse around the world if I have someone else to worry about?"

Hunter shrugs. "I can write anywhere in the world. I love traveling too. What places do you wanna see?"

"Remote places," I lie.

"They sound great. I've been to some of those places.

Wouldn't mind going again." He sits back in his chair, eyes on me, as if saying *what else?*

"I've finished. Thanks for cooking breakfast." He's so cocky, I don't want to admit how good the food is, however my sense of fairness wins.

He insists on carrying me out of the kitchen. This time, I don't bother arguing. Maybe because of that, for the first time, I'm aware of every single part of skin our bodies touch - the strength of his arms where they hold me, the barely there sensation of his hair touching my hands as they rest on the back of his neck.

I glance at his neck to distract myself and find something fascinating there, too. His Adam's apple is so pronounced I want to touch it.

It's a relief when Hunter deposits me on the couch. "Thank you." My voice is husky. I cough to dispel attention from how hoarse it is. I get Netflix ready. Nothing distracts me like a great film. I'm getting all thoughts of Hunter Wilson and his cocksure ways out of my head. His answer about being able to work anywhere makes way too much sense.

CHAPTER FOUR

Hunter

AFTER I'VE SETTLED Jasmine, I wash the dishes. I can't help thinking about our conversation. At twenty-two, I was still finding my way in the world, working every job that would take me to survive and send some money to Mom in Blossom Ford. If someone had suggested marriage, I would have told them to fuck off.

It wasn't until a couple of years later when I met Linda and Henry Franklin that I realized how beautiful love between two people who were fated could be. Till then, I'd always seen Mom struggle on her own to bring up me and my sister Eve. We were dirty poor even though Mom seemed to spend all day waiting tables.

Linda and Henry run a coffeehouse/reading library in Garnet City. Customers could read the books there for free while they drank coffee and ate the pastries

Linda was so good at making, but they couldn't take them home. Each wall of the building had shelves stacked to the brim with books the couple had accumulated or received as donations.

That's where I discovered how much I loved stories and that I could do something about the tales that had always formed in my head. Henry was a retired teacher who loved books and teaching. He found me reading a psychological thriller one day during my break and started asking me questions about what I loved and would improve about the book. Apparently, the writer was one of his favorites. At first I was annoyed. The man was my boss. I didn't want to socialize with him during break times, yet it wasn't long before I started looking forward to our conversations.

I'd always hated school and barely graduated high school before I left Blossom Ford, still I couldn't wait to talk about stories with Henry, as he insisted I call him.

Linda loved feeding people while Henry adored coaching. They weren't lucky enough to be blessed with children. They welcomed all lost souls like me, who crossed their path as family.

The doorbell rings. "Stay where you are. I'll get it," I say when I spot Jasmine reaching for her crutch.

"Morning." Cal is standing outside in his uniform, which is now rumpled.

I move aside and close the door after him.

"Cal, what the heck are you doing here? You just

finished your shift," Jasmine says.

"Jas, I'm hurt. Do you really think I would have gone home without checking on you? I can stay if you want me." He glances at me, then turns back to Jasmine.

"I'm perfectly fine. Thank you for checking up on me and calling last night. Now, go home and sleep."

He hands her a bag of what looks like doughnuts.

A grin splits her face. "You know me so well. Thank you again."

"Call if you need me."

Cal turns to leave and I uncoil myself from the door to the sitting room where I've been standing, watching them. I'm sure now the cop has feelings for Jasmine.

After I wave the cop off, I go to the kitchen and call the electricity company. Then I sit down with my laptop to work, but thoughts of Jasmine enter my mind. I give up. I'm way ahead of my deadline for the current book I'm working on anyway, so I'm not worried.

"Do you mind if I join you?" I ask her.

"Don't you have work?"

"I worked through the night."

"You can sleep. I'm fine."

"It hasn't been twenty-four hours yet. Besides, I'm used to going for a couple of days without sleep to complete a deadline."

"When this is finished, I'm switching to a romcom."

My lips tug up. I sit down on the chair closest to the

couch. "I get lots of ideas from romcoms."

"Are you able to watch a movie for fun or is your mind always analyzing the plot and searching for ideas to use in your books?"

"I've always loved movies and dramas that tell a good story. I still get involved in the drama, but you're right, I can't help noting things down I can use in a book. So, even watching movies is a little like working. My readers say my characters are emotionally complex. I think that's a direct effect of watching romcoms and romances."

"I suppose you watch them with your girlfriends."

"My mom and sister."

She looks at the screen. I force myself to glance away from her and do the same. When the credits roll, I realize nearly two hours have passed.

"You can choose the next film," Jasmine says so grudgingly I can't help chuckling.

"Are you worried you'll hate my choice or you're one of those people who likes to hog the remote control?"

"Both."

I chuckle again and settle into the chair. She's not getting rid of me that easily. "You can choose."

It's the kind of movie Mom and Eve like to watch. When Jasmine cracks up at a funny scene, I watch her and my heart stutters. The joy on her face is contagious. It warms me up.

At lunchtime, I throw some sandwiches together

and we eat them in the sitting room, with the glazed doughnuts as dessert.

She insists on helping with dinner, so I carry her back to the kitchen.

"Where did you learn to cook?" She asks as she chops onions.

"Mom was at work most of the time and would leave sandwiches or leftovers for us. Sometimes I fancied something hot, so whenever I could, I watched her cook. Once I learned a few dishes, I took over the cooking. I improvised a lot, so Mom and Eve, that's my sister, suffered a bit."

"Your mom was probably glad of the help." She smiles at me. "You must be the older sibling. My sister is ten years older than me; for a while she did most of the chores when I was little."

"Evie's younger," I agree.

I pick up the chopped carrots, wash them and put them in the pot of bean soup I'm making. It's a quick, nutritious dish that only takes half-an-hour to make.

"You're an excellent cook! This is delicious," Jasmine says after a mouthful. "I wonder if it'd taste as good if I make it."

"We can do it together until you get the hang of it, when your foot is better."

She asks me a question about a movie we watched earlier. And that's how we end up talking about movies for the rest of the evening until she dozes off.

I pick her up and head for the stairs. She's warm and

soft and awake.

"I like your Adam's apple," she says just before we reach the toilet.

I freeze. She traces her fingers down my throat and I feel it all the way in my cock.

"Jasmine." I can't help the growl in my low voice.

Her eyes leave my neck and collide with mine.

I lower my head and do what I've been wanting to do since I saw her at my place.

I kiss her.

Her lips are soft against mine. I nibble her slightly fuller bottom lip and her arms tighten around the back of my neck. I lift my head and stare at her. Her eyes are darker, and her lips are slightly open. This time, she's ready for me and kisses me as hard as I kiss her until we're both breathing hard.

I kiss her temple and place her on the floor outside the toilet, feeling the glide of her hands as she releases the back of my neck. Then I take a step from her. Because if I don't, I'll want so much more.

"I'll hobble to my bedroom when I finish."

I make sure she's safely inside the bathroom before I go down the stairs, wondering if Jasmine's injury and the happy family pictures dotted around the entire house will be enough to fight the temptation to walk into her room and make love to her.

CHAPTER FIVE

Jasmine

"HOW IS YOUR foot?" Hunter asks in the kitchen as he places a bowl of porridge in front of me.

He's wearing a thick, black turtleneck sweater paired with black jeans. It's criminal how good he looks.

"Pretty fine, considering I just walked down the stairs for the first time since the accident."

Hunter moved back to his place on Thursday and spent most of his time putting away belongings the removal company delivered. His electricity is back on too. Yet, he's spent every mealtime and evening at my place.

"You're glad right? If you'd put pressure on that ankle going up and down the stairs, you wouldn't be walking as well as you are now."

He's right, however, I'm out of sorts and he's the reason for it. I'm in no mood to admit how his superb care of me helped my body recover. Because while I'm well physically, mentally, I'm a wreck.

I don't know what possessed me to touch Hunter's Adam's apple that night. That episode ignited a passion I didn't know I had inside of me. During the day, I listen out for the sound of his voice telling me he's letting himself into the house and at night; I dream of him making love to me. I've only known him for a few days, yet l already I love the sound of his laughter, the way he taps his fingers when he's deep in thought and his favorite movies.

I would never have considered myself a psychological thriller reader, but after I asked about his writing on Thursday, he signed a book and gifted it to me. I totally surprised myself yesterday when I picked it up after lunch and was engrossed in it when he came in the evening to make dinner.

"Are you sure about returning to work tomorrow?" Hunter asks.

"I'll take my crutch just in case." There are some great-looking male doctors and nurses at the hospital. I need to be among them to see if what I've started to feel for Hunter is caused by close proximity. Maybe if I'm away from him, I won't crave him as much as I do now.

"Let me do the dishes," I say when we finish eating.

"I'll be back in a couple of hours. Make sure you wrap up." He looks at me, then lets himself out.

He has said nothing more about me being the woman of his life, though his gaze makes me feel branded. The tension between us is almost palpable. I'm glad I convinced him I'm well enough to go for a ride because I'm not sure I can be in the house with him without embarrassing myself by jumping his bones.

I bristle as Hunter checks me out before he deems I'm adequately wrapped, but deep down there's a warmth that has nothing to do with the layers of clothing I'm wearing.

"Are we ready?" I can't hide my excitement as he starts the bike after checking my helmet and putting on his own.

It's mid fall and there's a brisk wind in the hair. I hung on to Hunter and feel it whip my locs back as the powerful bike eats up miles of tarmac. It's as exhilarating as I thought it would be, and when Hunter switches off the engine at Blossom Ford Point, I'm a little sad.

I stand under the blossom tree and spread my arms wide, breathing in the pure cold air and the flowery scent all around me. My boots crunch leaves as I slowly make a full turn.

The sound of a camera going off makes my eyes open. Hunter snaps another picture with his cellphone.

I roll my eyes and stick my tongue out, the way I do for the kids at the ward. He snaps another picture, laughing.

Sometimes, I can't believe Hunter is thirty-seven years old. At moments like this, he seems so much younger.

I take one side of the blanket in his hands and together; we spread it on the floor. I peer into the picnic basket he made. There's a small bottle of wine besides the sandwiches, fruit, pots of yoghurt and water bottles.

"I bet you were prom king your senior year." I sip wine and watch him gulp back half a bottle of water.

"The opposite." He closes the lid on the bottle. "I hated school and had anger issues. I think I disliked not being able to help mom and had a chip on my shoulder about accepting charity. Some of my clothes were handouts from my friends' moms."

"Kids can be cruel."

"True. Nevertheless, it wasn't their fault Dad became ill and passed away soon after Evie was born. Once I got my head screwed on properly, I could appreciate the kindness of the Blossom Ford Community, however interfering they can be."

I laugh. "I hate how everyone gets involved in everyone's business. But I never want to live anywhere else, not long term."

"Me too," Hunter says softly, gray eyes on me.

My heart skips a beat. He's staring at me as if I were his prey. He leans towards me, plucks a purple leaf out of my hair.

"You're beautiful with this on your hair, by the way."

I lean over and do the same to him. "So do you."

"I want to kiss you."

"What are you waiting for?"

He kisses the corner of my mouth, but I want more. I turn and angle my head for a deeper kiss. He slides his tongue into mine and pushes me down onto the blanket. Sighing, I slide my hands through his hair.

It's amazing to have his body stretched out on top of me. His hands rove up and down the sides of my torso and hips.

"You smell so fucking good," he murmurs along my neck, dropping tiny kisses there.

I pull his head back to my mouth, unable to get enough of him. His kiss is like a drug I've become addicted to. Each pull of his tongue sends electricity to my core.

His hand finally grabs my breast through layers of clothing and a coat.

"Yes Hunter," I moan into his mouth.

He freezes. Lifts his head.

"What's the matter?" I want to relieve the frustration I've been suffering the last few days.

"Someone is coming this way."

"What?"

But then I hear it. The sound of barking.

Hunter sits and pulls me up, tucking a stray lock behind my ear. "Let's carry on when we have some privacy."

I nod, awed by the way he cares for me. The

chemistry between us is off the charts. I like so much about him; I think I'm falling in love.

CHAPTER SIX

Hunter

IT'S EARLY SUNDAY morning and I'm sitting in front of my doctor and friend Logan at his large private hospital in Garnet City.

"High tumor markers don't always mean cancer," he says.

"It may be."

"You're not experiencing any other symptoms, so the likelihood of that is very low. You must have a biopsy to know for sure. I can fit you in tomorrow, if you want it done as soon as possible."

"How long before the results are out?"

"I'll rush it. We should have the pathology report in a few days."

I wasn't expecting to be here; I think as I sit at a coffee shop after my appointment with Logan, unable to concentrate on work or anything else.

After our bike ride yesterday, I dropped Jasmine home and flew to Garnet City to meet my editor for a meeting regarding my next book. Before I arrived at our meeting point, I received a call from Logan asking me to see him at the hospital this morning.

I'd been a little worried. For the last five years, I've arranged for Mom, Evie, and me to have yearly check-ups. Apart from a callback for vitamins for Mom, Logan has never called any of us in. I didn't expect this.

Mom calls, but I mention nothing. She's visiting Evie. I don't want her or Evie to worry when this may just be a scare. Hearing Evie's husband and two boys in the background makes me smile.

I book myself into a hotel, but find it hard to sleep. After a night of tossing and turning, I crawl out of bed early and force myself to work, researching my next project. I want to hear Jasmine's voice, however the need to share what's happening with her is so strong; I can't take the chance of calling her.

The next morning, as I wait for the sedative I took for the biopsy to wear off, I wonder how cruel life can be sometimes. I finally found the woman of my dreams; yet, I might not spend my life with her because of cancer. There's no way I'd start something with Jasmine for her to suffer the way Mom did if I'm not around.

I fly back to Blossom Ford in the afternoon and take a taxi home. A cop's car is parked outside Jasmine's house. I wonder if Cal is inside when the door opens and the cop and Jasmine step out.

I get out of the taxi as Cal turns towards Jasmine, pulls her to him, and kisses her. Rage explodes inside me. I'm sprinting across the road and yard before I know it. Jasmine pushes Cal away a couple of beats before I reach him. It's not enough to curb my anger.

"Hunter…" Jasmine calls out.

I grab Cal and shove him further away from her. My hands fist. I use all the strength in me to stop myself from punching the younger man. Jasmine places her hand on my arm.

Cal grabs onto a post, his face ashen. He looks towards Jasmine. "I'm so sorry Jas. I don't know what came over me."

"I'll call you later," Jasmine says.

Cal looks to where her hand is holding onto mine, then turns and strides to his car. We stand on the porch until he's driven away.

"Are you okay?" I hold on to her shoulders and examine her. She looks a little dazed.

"Cal kissed me, I pushed him away. Nothing really happened."

"I saw it. Make sure you rest your ankle." I force my hands off her shoulders. "It's been a busy couple of days; I need sleep."

As I leave her house and walk to my yard, I can sense her eyes boring in to me. My head a mess, I grab a beer from the refrigerator and drink it in one go. I want to hug Jasmine, feel her warmth, and smell her heady fragrance. At night, I want to fuck her senseless, then sleep with her in my arms. I want to wake up with her and see all the places she wants to visit.

But how can I go to her now, when I might not stay in her life? Right now, I can't say I'll give her tomorrow, make any promises.

I grab another can of beer and down it quickly. When that doesn't destroy the wave of helplessness roiling inside me, I change into sweats and go jogging, setting a punishing pace. Maybe exhaustion will give me a reprieve from the anger and fear raging through me, even if it's only for a little while.

CHAPTER SEVEN

Jasmine

"GET A GOOD night's rest. You've been so distracted, if you carry on like this, you'll probably get a warning. You don't want that, not when you're still on probation," my colleague Sharon says as she drops me off after our shift.

"I will. Thanks." I wave her off and head to Hunter's place. There's no answer when I ring the bell. A string of curses slips out of me.

I take my phone out of my bag. There's no answer to the texts I sent him. No missed calls, either. His bike is in the yard, so he's not out riding.

The last three days since he walked off my porch, I've been mad. Even if he's tired or busy, he can still find time to send a quick text, surely. He admitted he saw what happened between Cal and me, so he must know I didn't kiss Cal back. He can't be angry about that.

Does he think I somehow encouraged Cal? Could he be blaming me for what happened? I shake my head and head home, completely at a loss.

When Cal popped in for a visit and confessed he was in love with me, I realized I'm in love with Hunter. I was scared that I had such powerful feelings for a man who's ready to settle down, yet I was excited too. Have I missed my chance with Hunter just like Cal missed his chance with me when I crushed on him in high school, but he wasn't into me? How could someone fall out of love in a couple of days? Perhaps what Hunter felt for me was lust.

I get out of my uniform, shower, and slip into comfortable clothes. I switch on the TV, but half of me is listening for movement next door. Because I'm starting to worry about Hunter. He's not the type to avoid things. If he's no longer in love with me or what happened with Cal is bothering him, he'd tell me.

It's only four o'clock, however it's already dark outside. I close the curtain, still now and then find myself flicking it open to see if Hunter's back.

A couple of hours later, I hear a car and head to the window. Hunter's getting out of a taxi. I rush to the door before I realize I'm in my socks. Quickly, I get my slippers and dash back to the front door. Only to see Hunter letting himself through my gate.

Hunter spots me and stops. Then he bolts toward me and picks me up. I squeak in surprise and grab onto his shoulders as he twirls, laughing.

My lips tug up. Relief floods through me. Hunter is fine.

Why didn't he reply to my messages and missed calls then?

As he slides me down his body, a flash of desire hits me. Ignoring it, I take a step back.

"What's going on?"

Hunter gives me that assessing glance that seems to take everything in. "You'll catch a cold." He grabs my hand, pulls me inside, and shuts the door.

"Well," I say once we're indoors and all he's doing is stare at me.

"I love you, Jasmine Williams!"

I want to tell him I love him too. "You were gone for three days. You didn't answer any of my calls or text back." I move away from him and cross my arms.

"I'm sorry. I'm trying to figure out how to explain the fucked-up situation I was in."

He sits on the sofa.

"You went to see your editor in Garnet City?"

Hunter sighs. I've never seen him looking so lost. He doesn't look like he's slept much.

I sit beside him. Take his hands in mine. "You're scaring me. I need to know what's happening."

"My doctor called while I was in Garnet City. My checkup showed increased tumor markers. I had a biopsy. It's negative, but it took a couple of days to get the results."

A heavy weight settles on my chest. Did he go through this alone? "Did you know this when you came back on Sunday?"

"I wanted to call, hear your voice. I just didn't want you worrying."

"Did you at least speak to your mom and sister?" Even as I ask, I know the answer.

He shakes his head. Stands up.

"Loving someone means going through pain with them. It hurts me more that I couldn't be there for you. What if the result were positive? Would you push me away?"

I see the answer in the hard set of his shoulders. "Hunter, you can't make that kind of choice for me."

He turns to me. "I can't put you through what my mom suffered."

"We can't control what'll happen. We can only be there for each other with all our might. Has your mom ever complained about loving your father? Of course, she would have been exhausted a lot, however did you ever feel she regretted caring for you alone?"

Hunter looks struck.

I stand up and close the distance between us. "I love you too. But I need to know if something happens, you'll trust me to go through it together, just like I'd trust you if I were ill or going through a difficult situation. That's what marriage is. Living through the good and bad together."

Hunter stares at me for a long time, gray eyes dark. His Adam's apple bobs up and down. "I can try," he finally says.

I wrap my arms around his waist. "That's good enough for now."

"I love the way you smell. I missed it and you so much." Hunter's arms close around me.

"You look like you haven't slept in days."

"There's something I want more than sleep right now."

Hunter lifts my head and presses his lips against mine. Hard. And just like that, I want him. I angle my head for a deeper kiss, but he pulls back.

"Not here, with your dad looking down on us."

I laugh as he grabs my hand and leads me across to his house.

As soon as we're indoors, he pushes me against the door and presses his lips to mine.

His mouth is like nectar. I can't get enough of kissing him. Every pull of his tongue sends shockwaves to my core. I tilt my head, wanting deeper into him, and glide my hands up and down his chest.

He grips my sweater and slides it up my body. I duck my head so he can slip it off. Then he takes my bra off, releasing my large breasts.

He sucks one nipple into his mouth and fondles the other, rolling it into a hard point. I clutch the door, desperately trying to hold myself up.

Hunter pulls harder. It feels so good I can't stop moaning.

"I've been dying to kiss you here. I can't wait to get inside you."

"Me too. If my panties get any wetter, I'm going to embarrass myself," I rasp.

"God Jasmine," Hunter growls. He moves away from me and shrugs off his coat, tosses it to the floor beside my top, his gray eyes smoldering.

I push my trousers and panties down and step out of them, unable to take my eyes off Hunter as he crouches to untie his bootlaces.

Shit, I'm getting wetter just looking at him.

He shucks off his trousers and lifts me, presses me back against the door. I wrap my legs around his waist. Sense him guiding his cock against my dripping pussy.

We both groan as Hunter drives the round tip of his cock forward.

"You feel so fucking good." He bites my neck. "Are you okay?"

I grasp his shoulders and roll my hips, trying to hurry him. "I need you all in."

I tug his head to me and slide my tongue into his mouth, getting drunk on the dancing of our tongues. He pulls back his hips and rams back in, again and again, setting a fast pace until all I can think about is Hunter.

Every thrust is heaven and drives me higher and higher. He strokes my clit and I cry out. My whole-body trembles as my core clenches around his shaft, waves of pleasure rolling through me.

He stills and grunts against my neck. A jet of hot cum fills me, intensifying the sensations inside my pussy.

"You're mine, Jasmine."

I lay my head against Hunter's chest.

He kisses me softly. "I want to do this with you every day."

"Against the door?"

"Nah, my legs won't cope, not every day. Besides, I want to take my time, taste every bit of you before I fuck you slowly."

"I won't say no to that."

EPILOGUE

Hunter

Six years later

I FINISH THE last revision on my manuscript, press save and email it to my editor. I roll my neck and stretch my shoulders.

My phone beeps.

"Got the manuscript. I need you to stay in the UK for a few more years. Your fans are going crazy over the new series you're setting there."

I chuckle. "Roman, you know I have a family, right?"

"Your beautiful wife won't mind."

"I'll take lots of pictures. Just like I did in Qatar. My beautiful wife will be home from work any time now so, take care." I hung up the phone and stand up, just as a bark sounds.

I walk through the open door of my study, in the cottage Jasmine and I are renting, to the living room.

Our son Olly stands in his cot, arms pushing through the spaces between the bars to pet Baxter, our spaniel. He puts up his chubby arms when he sees me.

"Daddy!" He jumps up and down.

"Did you have a good sleep?" I carry him out and kiss his cheek before I put him on the floor beside Baxter, who's shaking his tail.

"Mommy," Olly says.

"Let's go wait for her."

It's early fall. It's already cold in Southeast England. I put a jacket over Olly's baby grow and a pair of sneakers on his tiny feet. The smell of the sea hits me as we step outside and I sit on the wooden bench in our front yard. Baxter runs around in circles and Olly chases him, trying to catch his tail.

I spot Jasmine and watch her run the rest of the way home. Baxter and Olly throw themselves at her, making her laugh out loud. She crouches and pets them until a seagull cries overhead and they stare up at it, pointing excitedly.

She comes and sits on my lap. I pull her closer and kiss her.

"We're going to scare Mrs. Green again," she says when we come up for breath.

"The next time we move, we're getting a house in the middle of nowhere."

Jasmine chuckles and sits beside me.

"Did you finish revising your manuscript?" she asks.

"I emailed it. Roman wants us to stay here for a long time."

"I'm so happy moving has improved your career. You're becoming even more of an international star. First in Qatar, now here."

We married a year after we met and left for Qatar a year after that, when Jasmine found a nursing post there. Our boy was born in the US before we moved out here. I've loved every bit of our lives. Finding my soulmate and living with her is better than what I'd dreamed.

"You, Olly and Baxter are the reason I've become more successful." I look over to check on Olly. He's only fifteen months old, but he can already run a few laps round the yard. "Are you sure you won't miss this wandering life when we return home next year?"

"I loved the two years we spent in Qatar, just the two of us. I'm having a ball working here but I want Olly to grow up and go to school in Blossom Ford with his grandparents. It'll be easier for him to see his cousins, too. We can always travel later, when he's in college."

I nod, full of optimism for the life ahead of us. Sometimes I get scared, however I live each day to the fullest. I call Olly and Baxter, and we head inside for Jasmine to shower and change before we go on our usual walk along the beach.

The End

MARRYING THE WIDOWED DOCTOR

CURVY BRIDES OF BLOSSOM FORD #5

Liam

I USED TO think middle age crisis was an excuse to do crazy things. However, I'm starting to believe it is a thing. Nothing else, rational that is, can explain the fact that I'm considering marrying a woman matched to me by a matchmaking agency, only a few days after my forty-first birthday. Especially when the woman I loved and built a family with has only been gone three and a half years.

My hands tighten around a smiling picture of Lucy, taken before our marriage, her auburn hair flying and once again the certainty that I have to follow through with this marriage, however crazy it is, solidifies in me. I have to keep the promise she forced me to make on our wedding night; I would find someone to love and be a mom for our children if anything happened to her.

Loving is out of the question. Never again do I want to go through the agonizing pain of losing a woman I love. Besides, even if it's possible to fall in love again, how can I live with the kind of happiness I shared with Lucy when she's not here?

I can, however, fulfill the mom part.

"Daddy, Ollie is pulling my hair." Olivia hides behind me as her twin brother chases her.

I place the picture on a shelf and pick up my four-year-olds, one on each arm. They give me the strength to keep the silly promise I made. I first started thinking about marriage when the twins were three and turned into monsters. Their nanny fell pregnant and quit to be a full-time mum.

None of the nannies that came afterwards could control them or deal with the uncertainty of the long hours I worked, when urgent surgeries became necessary. Then a couple of weeks ago, during Christmas dinner at Lucy's parents in New York, Olivia declared Santa was bad because he hadn't provided the first present on her list–a mom.

I want to do everything I can to make Liv and Ollie happy. That's what I'll focus on. It's the only way to make sense of me going ahead with an arranged marriage.

The bell rings.

"Be nice to the lady and each other." I place the kids on the floor beside a pile of toys. Squaring my shoulders, I march to the door and open it.

The smile of welcome freezes on my face. My breath hitches. Large sea-green eyes set in an oval-shaped face with the most kissable lips I've ever seen stare up at me for what seems like ages before I realize I'm staring back. The picture the agency sent didn't do justice to the curvy woman standing in the cold. The honey of her cheeks and the black of her long coat give the snow-covered garden color.

"Miss. Clark?"

She nods.

I move aside to let her pass, then take her coat. In tight-fitting black jeans and a red blouse that complements smooth honeyed skin, her curves are even more alluring. So is the scent of roses coming from her. My cock stirs.

Calm down and breathe.

I hung up the coat, and stride to the sitting room, annoyed at my reaction. It's unwanted and improper. In the last three and a half years, I've come across many attractive women, yet I never showed the slightest interest. Why now when I'm about to check whether Angel Clark would make an excellent mother for my kids?

The moment she spots the twins, she heads straight for them, sits cross-legged on the floor near them and says hi.

They watch her. A couple of minutes pass. Ollie traipses to her. Grabs her ponytail with his chubby hands and pulls. Angel reaches for him, tickles until he's giggling and releases her hair. He falls onto her lap, squirming.

"That's the consequence of pulling my hair. I won't stop tickling." There is laughter in Angel's face and her hands are gentle.

My lips tug up when Liv moves closer to the duo on the floor, hazel eyes identical to her brother's wide.

"Are you big sister Liv?" Angel asks.

Olivia nods.

"I'm Miss. Angel." She stretches out a hand.

Liv's eyes move from the hand to Ollie, who's still sitting on Angel's lap, then back to the hand. She shakes it.

Warmth spreads through my chest. Ollie and Liv fight like cats and dogs, but Liv is very protective of her brother. Although they are only a few minutes apart, he's developing at a much slower pace than her. Pleasing him is one way to get on her good side.

"He's Ollie." Liv sits in front of Angel, copies her cross-legged pose and studies her.

"I have to talk to Miss Angel, so come and draw," I say to the twins after they've had a little chat with Angel.

I settle Liv and Ollie in the kitchen with crayons and drawing pads. When I return to the sitting room, Angel is gazing at the photos spread all over the room of me and Lucy with the kids at different ages. In the most recent picture, the twins are six months old.

I sit and switch the monitor to listen to the kids, but my eyes stray to Angel as soon as I'm done.

"I love Liv and Ollie," she says once she joins me in the sitting area.

That is something I like about her. How direct and decisive she is, despite being only twenty-four. I noticed it in her short profile statement and that, together with the fact she stated she's more interested in being a full-time mom rather than having a husband, is the reason I chose her. Her experience as a childcare provider is a bonus I'm grateful for.

"They like you. They rarely take to strangers. What do you think about the marriage now?"

A blush tints her cheeks, making me wonder what she's thinking. She turns away and studies a picture of the kids.

"I'll go ahead." She gazes at me, but I can't make the expression in her eyes.

"We have a deal, then."

Most of the paperwork for preparing the marriage, including a contract, was done online. She wanted to meet Liv and Ollie, and I had to see how the three of them interacted before making a final decision and signing the contract.

As the kids and I see angel out, I remind myself why I'm marrying her—to get a mom for my kids. the reason I couldn't stop my eyes from watching the way her ass fit those tight jeans as she put her coat on was the three and a half years of celibacy my body endured. I may not be able to control the way I react to angel, but that's okay, because my heart suffered so much after losing lucy, it knows not to fall in love again.

MATCHED TO PATRICK

THE O'CONNORS OF BLOSSOM FORD #1

Patrick

MINGLED LAUGHTER DRIFTS from the sitting room, bringing mixed feelings of joy and sadness. We decorated the entire house in green–it's St Patrick's Day. As usual, we've been to church and are now having beef pot roast, which Mom and Aunt Shauna insist on making every year on the feast day of St. Patrick. Dad would have been so happy to hear that laughter. Even though we gathered like today at Christmas, St Patrick's Day was his favorite holiday.

I remove more salad from the refrigerator.

"Ready for the parade of women our moms no doubt have lined up for you this year?" My cousin Lorcan asks. I know his lilting voice like I know my own.

I snap the refrigerator closed. "Will I be the only one on display?"

He winces. "You're the eldest. And you're Aunt Caitlin's only son, so you'll definitely be in the firing line. Mom will surely want to marry Riordan off first. I'll be an afterthought."

The lump in my throat prevents me from chuckling. I can't really blame Lorcan. I used to be like him. The thought of marriage drove me barmy. Not anymore.

At first I couldn't imagine myself being happy with a family, not with the crushing guilt I felt over what happened to Little Fiona. Before Dad passed, he made me promise to let go of that guilt and cherish the time I've been blessed with. Although I believed it'd never happen, little by little, I'm appreciating life.

I want what Mom and Dad had, though. They were meant for each other. Someone out there is my soulmate and the moment I find her, I'm not letting go. For the last couple of years, Mom and Aunt Shauna's matchmaking efforts haven't bothered me in the least.

I glance outside to where Riordan, my cousin and Lorcan's eldest brother, sits in the spring sun. "Riordan is not ready to get married. I doubt he'll hang around for the picnic and anyone our moms might want to set him up with."

That giant of a man is still blaming himself for what happened to his little sister Fiona, even though it's been twenty-six years since she was taken from us. Our dads were first cousins -both O'Connors. The two of us are forty-four, but I'm older than Riordan by one week. As the oldest children in the O'Connor family, it was our responsibility to make sure Fiona was safe.

Lorcan opens the back door.

"Mom is calling," he says to Rio.

It's the only thing that'll move my eldest cousin. Aunt Shauna may not be calling him now, but Riordan knows she'll soon be, wanting to make sure he spends as much time with us as possible before he scoots up the mountain.

Riordan and Lorcan's six brothers and Dad are watching TV while Mom and Aunt Shauna are chat.

"Don't forget to take good care of my friend Nara when she gets here. She was very kind to me the other day in town when I forgot my wallet," Mom reminds me.

We spend another couple of hours leisurely drinking and chatting, then get up to prepare for the outdoor picnic, which starts at four. The whole town is invited to our farm. Our parents started the tradition a few years after settling in Blossom Ford and starting a lettuce farm together, because they missed spending St Patrick's Day with their large family back in Ireland.

We put up tents on the large grass area between my house and Riordan's. Mom and Aunt Shauna used to do all the food when they were younger, but now, Lorcan gets caterers in to bring sandwiches and other finger food. By the time the townsfolk arrive, Cormac and Emmet, my youngest cousins, have set up a DJ stand which is playing upbeat music and the entire field is filled with green bunting and balloons.

I'm taking a breather from greeting people when I see a woman strolling towards Mom. Something about the way she walks catches my attention. She's wearing black skinny jeans that mold her curvy ass to perfection and a light green top that covers a pair of generous breasts and complements the sun-kissed tone of her skin. Wavy jet-black hair falls below her shoulders and shimmers in the sun.

I'm too far away to see the color of her eyes. Before I know it, I'm marching towards Mom, curiosity and something I can't name, compelling me forward.

"I'm so glad you came, Nara," Mom is saying when I reach her side on a strategic part of the field where she, Aunt Shauna, and their friend Ms. Penny can see everyone.

Tawny, that's the color of her eyes.

I answer myself as Nara greets everyone with an amiable smile that reaches her almond-shaped, yellow-brown eyes and warms the inside of my chest. She's comfortable around Mom, Aunt Shauna and their friends, even though she must be in her mid-twenties. The silver hoops on the tops of her ears glint in the sunshine.

"This is my son, Patrick." Mom points to me.

I stretch out my hand in greeting and when she holds mine; hers is small and smooth against my large and calloused one. I don't let go and she glances up at me.

That's when I know. That I've found the woman I've spent the last few years searching for.

The friendly warmth on her face is replaced by something else: interest. A tinge of pink fills her cheeks before she pulls her hand away.

Her voice cracks a little when she says hello leaving me to wonder where the confidence she exhibited a few moments ago went.

"I'll show you where the food is," I say.

"I don't want to trouble you." She looks about her. "I'll find it, thank you."

"It's no trouble at all," Mom beams at Nara. "Patrick will walk you over to the food area. Just ask him if there's anything you need to know."

A frown forms on my face as I lead the way. At my age, I'm old enough to know when a woman has the hots for me. I know Nara fancies me, but she's decided not to pursue it.

If there's one thing I'm good at, is getting to the root of a problem. Now I've found Nara, I'll have to convince her I'm the only man for her.

OTHER BOOKS BY THE AUTHOR

CURVY BRIDES OF BLOSSOM FORD SERIES

MARRYING THE PROTECTIVE PROFESSOR

MARRYING THE GRUMPY DIRECTOR

MARRYING THE POSSESSIVE NEIGHBOR

MARRYING THE WIDOWED DOCTOR

MARRYING THE SCARRED SOLDIER

MARRYING THE OBSESSIVE CEO

MARRYING THE BIG MOUNTAIN MAN

THE O'CONNORS OF BLOSSOM FORD SERIES

MATCHED TO PATRICK

ABOUT THE AUTHOR

Iris West writes short and spicy romance about alpha heroes and the women they can't help falling in love with. She loves reading all types of romance books that have a happy ending and is an avid Kdrama fan.

Follow or like her on Facebook and Goodreads.

FREE BOOK

Would you like a free book? Sign up to my mailing list at https://dl.bookfunnel.com/t191w45ryj to receive a copy of Loving My Fake Husband, a free to subscribers only, Curvy Brides of Blossom Ford Series short story.

HELP OTHERS FIND THIS BOOK

Thank you for reading Marrying The Possessive Neighbor. If you enjoyed this book, please help others discover it by leaving a review at your favorite online book store.

Many thanks,

Iris xx